Dedicated
all the fraud fighters
around the world.

A is for Account Takeover

Account Takeover is when a fraudster steals your online account information and pretends to be you.

To play a game online, you have to create an account in your name with a password you think up. Fraudsters want that information to break into accounts to steal money.

B is for Bot

A Bot is software designed by fraudsters used to conduct a gazillion attacks on a gazillion online accounts.

The word bot sounds a little bit like the word robot, doesn't it? But these aren't like Transformers. Bots make stealing money super fast and hard to detect, which makes it hard to stop them.

C is for Credential Stuffing

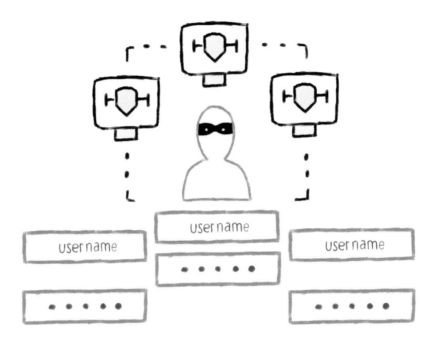

Credential Stuffing is when fraudsters use millions of stolen online credentials to get into accounts.

Your name, email address and passwords you use to create online accounts are your personal information. Fraudsters want that information to pretend to be you and login to accounts to steal money.

D is for Deep Fake

Deep Fake is when a fraudster creates a video that looks like someone said something they didn't.

Fraudsters create deep fake videos usually to spread lies. The videos look like a celebrity or politician, but it is really someone else.

E is for Emulator

An Emulator is a software technology that makes one computer look like another computer.

An emulator enables fraudsters to get around security controls that can identify "good" devices from "bad" devices. This helps them avoid detection when committing crimes.

F is for Fraudster

A Fraudster is a bad person who steals money from honest people and businesses.

Fraudsters use your personal information so that they can pretend to be you online and take money that doesn't belong to them or items they can sell for money.

G is for Gift Card Fraud

Gift Card Fraud is an easy way for fraudsters to steal cash.

Fraudsters go to stores and write down the numbers of a bunch of gift cards, then continually check online to see if they have been activated. If so, they spend them. Not very nice!

H is for Hoarding

Hoarding is when a fraudster uses bots
to buy up popular items or tickets.

Buying up all of the hot items, like shoes, concert tickets,
video games or airplane seats and reselling them or driving
prices up for other people is a common type of fraud.

I is for Identity Theft

Identity Theft is when a fraudster pretends to be you online.

Fraudsters steal your identity by using your picture, social security number, email address, and birth date. They pretend to be you while they commit crimes online.

J is for Javascript Injection

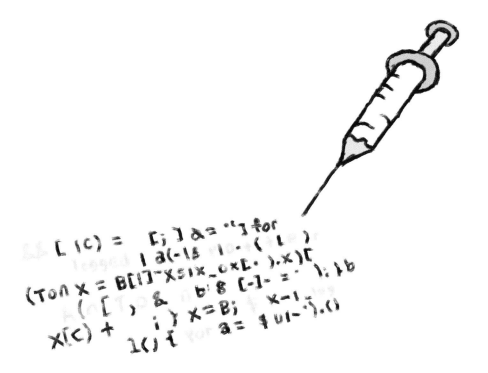

Javascript Injection makes one website look like another website.

A fraudster uses a javascript injection to change a business's website design, grab important information from the website, and even hack into the business's other systems.

K is for Keylogging

Keylogging is a set of instructions that fraudsters create and download on your computer, iPad, or mobile phone.

Keylogging is like someone spying on your computer and mobile device keypad to watch the letters and numbers you touch, when accessing your online accounts, so they can learn your password.

L is for Loan Fraud

Loan Fraud is when a grown-up lies on a loan application.

When a grown-up buys a house, they have to get a loan called a mortgage. If they write on the loan application that they earn more money than they really do, that's not telling the truth and is loan fraud.

M is for Money Mule

A Money Mule isn't an animal. It is a real person being used to move stolen money.

Money mules aren't necessarily bad people. They are often tricked by fraudsters to help them transfer the money fraudsters have stolen from an online account.

N is for New Account Fraud

New Account Fraud happens when a fraudster opens an online account as somebody else.

Doing this, they are able to spread lies to other people, open credit cards under a fake name, and steal money without getting in trouble for it.

O is for Online Scam

An Online Scam is any type of attack that occurs on the internet.

An online scam happens on a device, like a laptop, mobile phone, or tablet. Account takeover is an example of an online attack (see A is for Account Takeover).

P is for Phishing

Phishing is when a fraudster sends you a text or email asking questions about your identity.

Fraudsters use phishing to get people's information to later use for stealing money or someone's identity. They might send you an email that looks like it is coming from someone you know, asking you to click a link.

Q is for Quality Score

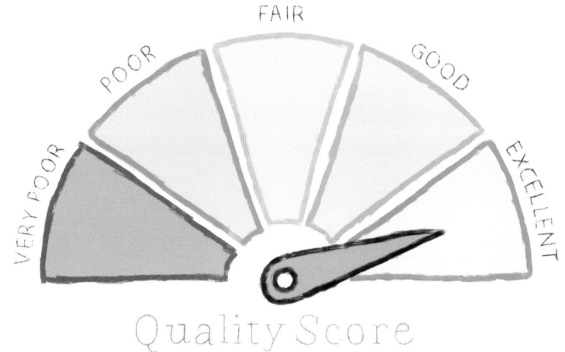

Quality Score is like a grade you get in school that tells whether a person is good or bad.

Quality score is used to tell whether someone online is a regular person or a fraudster trying to attack someone on the computer. This score can warn businesses so that they can stop fraudsters from attacking.

R is for Romance Scams

Romance Scams are when a fraudster acts like they want to be your girlfriend or boyfriend online.

Fraudsters steal a real person's name and picture from social media and pretend to be your special friend. After they make you feel warm and fuzzy inside, they will ask to borrow some money that they won't return.

S is for Social Engineering

Social Engineering is when a fraudster tricks a person into handing over personal information.

Fraudsters use social engineering methods through emails, in social media messages, and even over the phone. Fraudsters play on your trust and the fact that most people want to help other people. Phishing (see P is for Phishing) is a type of social engineering.

T is for Trained Bot

A Trained Bot is a bot that's been taught how to hack into online accounts.

Companies protect online accounts by putting puzzles in place that make it hard for bots to get inside. Knowing this, fraudsters will teach bots how to do those puzzles so they can hack into accounts and steal money.

U is for Utility Scam

A Utility Scam is when a fraudster gets TV, electricity, and more by pretending to be someone else.

Fraudsters will sign up for cable TV, gas for heating their house, or electricity by pretending to be a responsible person. While fraudsters gets to watch their favorite tv show for free, the company charges the person they are pretending to be.

V is for Vishing

Vishing is when a fraudster calls someone on the phone for personal information.

Fraudsters will pretend to be from a company, the government, or a friend and make up a reason for the person to send them money. For instance, the fraudster might pretend they are from a TV company and say the person they are calling forgot to pay their bill.

W is for Work-From-Home Scam

A Work-From-Home Scam offers you a fake job that says you'll make a lot of money fast.

Usually work-from-home scams require a person to do simple tasks with the promise of being paid a lot of money. This is just a way the fraudster can steal money from you, saying that you need to pay for something first or charging a fee to be hired.

X is for X-Border Fraud

X-Border Fraud is a scam that crosses over many different countries or states.

Often fraudsters persuade a person to send money or expensive items to other countries. Fraudsters convince people to send money quickly through their bank and since it goes to a different country, it's really hard to get back.

Y is for High Yield Investment Fraud

High Yield Investment Fraud is a promise to make a lot of money in return for less money.

Fraudsters will ask people to give them money and promise they will get a lot of money back in the future. People are willing to spend a small amount of money to get rich down the line, but fraudsters never keep their promises.